Sam Smith started writing business after going through a series of changes and challenges in her life, her writing reflects hidden problems in society which have somehow been ignored. Her writing style is simple and readers could walk with her during observations and have a closer look at the issues we are scared to address or choose not to pay attention to them. Reading her books could be a ringing bell to the ears of those who could avoid such problems and those who never think they could be the next victim.

Sam Smith

Listen to Shoes

Austin Macauley Publishers™
London • Cambridge • New York • Sharjah

This is a work of fiction. Names, characters, businesses, places, events, locales, and incidents are either the products of the author's imagination or used in a fictitious manner. Any resemblance to actual persons, living or dead, or actual events is purely coincidental.

Ordering Information
Quantity sales: Special discounts are available on quantity purchases by corporations, associations, and others. For details, contact the publisher at the address below.

Publisher's Cataloging-in-Publication data
Smith, Sam
Listen to Shoes

ISBN 9781685623746 (Paperback)
ISBN 9781685623753 (ePub e-book)

Library of Congress Control Number: 2023905111

www.austinmacauley.com/us

First Published 2023
Austin Macauley Publishers LLC
40 Wall Street, 33rd Floor, Suite 3302
New York, NY 10005
USA

mail-usa@austinmacauley.com
+1 (646) 5125767

I step out of the subway station. It is freezing. In a minute, I feel small portions of my body start to freeze; my feet, my fingers go numb. While I am struggling to find a slightly warmer place, I notice a body in an old torn blanket in front of me. I try to not look at him. I don't know if I am scared of being the next victim of the economic recession, begging for a piece of bread after my savings are gone, or if it's the crazy weather that makes me turn my head away. I'm not alone; I am watching all kinds of people passing and not even looking at him.

I run to the bus station. At least there, under a roof, I will be protected from snow. I sit on a bench inside the station, but it is colder than ice. I am wearing jeans and a winter jacket – nothing very special – and my shoes are cheap sneakers from Walmart. I can't see what shoes that man who is lying down on the street is wearing; his blanket completely covers him. I look at the other passengers' shoes; they are talking. A girl in her twenties is wearing long boots with high heels; they look very warm. Before I look at her face, I try to listen to her shoes. They are saying, "I hate this weather and instead of sitting in her car that was in the repair shop, I have to wait here." One of the shoes says it will need polishing as soon as they get home and this is the last time she will be standing in this crazy weather. I am watching them move far away from the bench and while they are going, I look at their owner. She is wearing a hat, a scarf, and a nice jacket. I wonder why she isn't taking a taxi; in a few minutes, she is in her taxi and on her way home. My chin is down, just trying to kill time without thinking about my feet that are almost frozen.

A pair of sneakers come inside the station. They are old and look as if they have been used for a long time. Compared to them, my shoes are princesses. These are black and flat; one heel is almost gone. It shows that their owner has been wearing them while walking for quite a time. I turn my eyes from her shoes to her face; she is a woman in her 50s who looks tired and is carrying a big bag as if she is taking some leftover lunch to her family. I try to guess what her job could be. Her jacket shows that she has tailored it by herself, or at least someone who is not very good at design has done so. She is wearing a red knitted hat that doesn't match her jacket or shoes. In her hand is a paper ticket, which shows she is not very familiar with technology or doesn't have a pass card. She tries to sit on that freezing bench, but like me, after a few minutes she changes her mind. I walk out of the station to look at the bus schedule. It shows that there won't be any buses for at least the next 20 minutes. Immediately, that body on the street comes to mind, but I don't let him stay; I push him out. No, I will not think about that. It's not me, not even that woman with the old shoes. I will buy a new pair of shoes tomorrow, I can afford it; I will not let myself go. *I shouldn't, I won't*; I repeat this several times.

I try to look at better shoes now. I feel sick and cold in my stomach. I turn my head to the other side of the line-up, but it isn't nicer than what I have already seen. Most of these people are standing in this messed-up weather because they can't afford a taxi or a car; why should their shoes be better than that other woman, or me?

It's as if ice is growing from the ground into my shoes and coming up into my legs. I start to walk, but I can hear shoes are talking; they sound very loud inside my head. I hold myself tight. *Shut up, I don't want to hear what you say.* But for some reason, I notice something in their owners' eyes; that they are asking me to listen to their shoes. One pair of shoes is laughing and making fun of a pair of high-heeled shoes in this icy situation; they are flat and wide, and the owner is in his 30s. He is saying to his pair, "Look at those high heels; they make a sexy noise, but I doubt they can make it to that bus." He is laughing so hard that I feel as if he is going to tear himself apart in a few minutes. His pair of shoes is listening with a smile, as if they approve of their partner's idea but don't want to interrupt him. In front of them there is a very happy pair in a mixture of blue and red, not quite flat; they look okay but still not very suitable for this weather. I turn my eyes from them to their owner's face. He is a teenage boy; he looks very energetic and can't stay still in one place, and all the time he is talking into his cell phone. I am sure he spends most of his allowance on his phone. He is the type of guy who doesn't care what the weather is like; a typical teen. I guess he wears the same shoes in summer too, but his shirt and black jacket are very fashionable; he might be part of the group that have to take the bus because he doesn't want his parents to give him a ride in their car.

The clock on my phone shows we still have to wait another 10 minutes. I can't stay any longer; I look through the glass door inside the subway station. It is crowded but still has some space for standing. I run back inside; it is way warmer than outside. I look around to see if I can find a seat. Some passengers are sitting on the benches and have left their bags on the next seat. I think, *how selfish*, but I am sure they think they are tired and have to take at least two seats. They must think they are the only ones who are tired and need a job, and attention. While I am standing, they look me up and down from head to toe, as if they are trying to say, *your clothes look good; you don't need to sit. You don't even deserve to be inside.* In a moment, I think that guy on the street had been subjected to the same judgment and no one paid attention to him, probably because he didn't sit on two seats.

I walk close to the window to make sure I am not missing the bus. I have already swiped my card and I don't want to pay extra to stay in this weather and get charged twice. This man in the blanket doesn't leave me alone; I can't see his face or even his feet, I just guess he is a man. Before, he was young, was working, and had a family, and now he is lying on the street and not even passengers want to look at him. He might not be alive by tomorrow or the day after, and no one will know about his death.

In my head, I repeat, *I will buy good shoes tomorrow.* My shoes will tell people how their owner was active, respected; and they'll never say I lost everything years ago. They will be proud of me. It is like those kids who are scared of the dark and try to get over it by singing. I look at my shoes. They look okay; no one knows how much I paid for them or how warm they are. I am good, no worries. During those challenges, I see a blue bus stopped in front of the station. I run outside and wait in line. This line makes me feel sad. Their shoes, their shoes are killing me. Some of them are crying, I can hear them. A woman in her 40s is wearing flip-flops in this crazy snowy weather; her white open shoes show her cold feet, with black fabric pants and a long blue jacket. OMG, even looking at her makes me feel cold. I let her get on the bus, and then an overweight man with a cane who is dragging one of his legs. His shoes are big and black; his shoe size is probably14 or more. I think his feet could be able to take his weight.

I don't know why, but when I am on the bus, I try to find a good warm pair of shoes on the street. I sit in a window seat. The glass is steamy because of the different temperature between the inside and outside, but I get a blurry view. I am searching, and suddenly, I see a pair of boots. I just focus on these boots before I look at their owner. They are black with long shoelaces. I saw this before; it looks like the shoes of a soldier or someone in the military. The steps are strong; my eyes go up from his shoes to his pants and jacket. He is wearing a safety vest. I knew it; he must be part of a construction or safety team. I realize he has a job, warm boots, and a safety vest. Good for him, he is standing on the curb.

The bus slowly moves and the ice on my feet and hands is melting. I know I have to get off the bus at last station and wait for another bus. It is getting dark, and the street is being covered with snow. I think this woman with the flip-flops will lose her feet tonight. I turn my head and look around; some of the passengers are sleep, some look very tired and some, like me, sit up straight to make sure their shoes are not embarrassed.

I step out of bus at last station. It is completely dark; the station is not as busy as it was this afternoon. Most of the shoes are in shoe boxes or lined along corridors, talking about their day, but my shoes are still shaking in this freezing weather. At least this station has a waiting room and some heaters that are not working properly. I move myself under one of the ceiling heaters. I feel some warm wind flowing on the top of my head, but my feet are still very cold. My shoes look at me tired and disappointed; they try to remind me of when I first tried them on. In Walmart, they were beautiful and new, but now some white spots are on top of their uppers; it is from the salt that is used to melt ice. One side of the left shoe is close to being torn, and I am the only one who knows what is going on inside them. When I take them off, I can see how damaged they are. I want to say something to make them feel better, but I don't really have anything to say. I think if I can't save my shoes, at least I should save my gloves.

After a few minutes, my eyes can see, there is a pair of shoes inside the station; a pair of shiny brown shoes. They are walking around as if they are monitoring everything. A pair of flat boots that look very warm and comfy, a pair of brand sneakers full of white spots that seems to have walked a long way, and an old pair of black shoes sit under one of the benches. A few shoes are outside, and I can't see them very well. For some strange reason, I am interested to know about those shiny brown shoes. I follow them all over the station. They can't stay in one place; it's like they are running from something. After five minutes watching them dancing from this side to that, I try to look at their owner. He is wearing gray fabric pants with a warm hat, gloves and a long overcoat; his appearance suggests he works for the government. When I look at him, he turns his eyes away, like a kid who has done something, and when you catch him, he tries not look at you. His shoes show he didn't walk in the snow or found himself in a bad situation; he must have got to the station by a private car or taxi. Why is he here? I am searching in my head to find a reason. I realize that most of the time I have seen brown shoes, I have felt they were following me, like their mission is spying or monitoring. I am not wrong; his shoes definitely show he is not the type of person who normally takes the bus. He has probably parked his car in the parking lot back of the station and is here for a specific reason.

I look around. There are not any interesting shoes around. The warm boots are on the feet of a girl who looks like a student and is probably coming back from university or her dorm to visit her family. Those old shoes belong to a woman who is sitting on the corner bench and completely out of the world; she must have had a very bad and hard day. The sneakers belong to a tall man who looks too busy to care about those spots on his shoes; he could afford another pair if necessary, and then there are my shoes; are those brown shoes after my shoes?

I pause for a while. I am very sure I have seen shiny brown shoes many times. One pair in hospital belonged to a tall man with a nice outfit; something about the way he spoke impressed me. He was wearing brown shiny shoes. Another pair, in the office, was on the feet of a well-dressed man with a dark brown jacket and light brown pants. There was something about his walking; his step was strong and made a ringing noise. They all had something in common; they cared about their appearance. Why is this one here? He is not taking a bus with any of us.

At this moment, I see that the last bus is here. I pull my hat down to protect my ears and step out of the station. Other than me, there is just one more passenger on the bus and none of those passengers in the station join my ride. Through the bus window, I try to follow those brown shoes. I can't see them; my angle is not good for observing what is going on in the station. Whatever. There are a million other shoes; I can listen to them, I think.

The driver stays for a few moments to make sure there are no more passengers for the last bus and then slowly moves. It is crazy outside. I am wondering if the man with brown shoes is driving his car. His car must be a four-wheel drive and is probably an SUV. It is impossible that any other type of car could get to destination without having an accident. I can't see the other passenger's shoes. He is behind me and I don't want to scare him by turning my head to watch his feet. "When my shoes step out of the bus to walk from the bus station to my apartment, they will meet other shoes, if any pair is outside at this time and temperature," I say to myself.

I hop off the bus. My shoes almost drown in the dirty, melting snow at the bus station. I can see they are wet, tired, and angry. One of them yells at me, "Ooohhhh, be careful, can't you step somewhere a little dryer? I am not your slave, you know?" I hear him but prefer not to say anything. I am as angry as he is. I remember my expensive beautiful shoes. They were sitting on racks inside my walk-in closet, and I could use any pair I like, depending on the weather and situation. In my head, I say to those shiny brown shoes, “Your shoes are nothing compared with what I had.” After this conversation and rubbing my previous shoes in the brown shoes’ face, I feel better.

While I am talking in my head, I have already passed half of the way. My face is red and my nose is numb. I have totally forgotten about my wet shoes. I hear the noise of some other shoes that are walking but I am too cold to look at them. I increase my speed and take longer and stronger steps. No one can know how my shoes feel.

In my apartment, I take off my shoes, they are whining. I promise I will clean them tomorrow. I need to go to bed to make myself ready for another day. In the morning, every time I see my shoes, the image of that man in the blanket is in my head. That’s it, I am going shoe shopping today. I clean and wear them again. My pants are long enough to cover the uppers; this way, they stay warmer, and the white spots are covered up.

In the mall, I look for the shoe store. I know many of them; I even know where they are located. I used to look for my favorite brands and styles and used to try on many pairs. I sit on a bench inside to take a breath. Either my age, the winter or thinking about my shoes has made me short of breath. While I am sitting there, I look at hundreds of shoes that are walking around. Most of them look happy, as if their owner has taken them to Disneyland; they are playing, laughing, and talking aloud. The noise they make sounds like a whistle in my ears. I don’t want to look at the shoes’ owners’ faces, just the shoes.

I pick myself up and take off my gloves, hat, and jacket. I feel lighter; this way, I don't have to put lots of weight on my shoes. Inside the mall there is a warm and happy environment. In some parts of it, you can smell freshly baked food. It makes me feel younger; it might be related to those years of wearing good shoes.

I walk to one of my favorite shoe stores. It is like you are watching jewelry; they are beautiful. In one row, those expensive, high-end shoes are sitting beside each other. You can't wear them for taking the bus or walking on the street; they are used for parties, weddings, and probably for hosting your friends when you want to show them your taste. In another row, they are tall and ankle boots. They could be a good choice, but their price is out of my budget. In the middle, you can find a mixed set of shoes, from summery sandals to warm comfy shoes. I think I can afford one pair of them, but then I would have to pay for a more expensive outfit, hat, and gloves. What about a few months from now? I need my money for food and other expenses. I look at my shoes again. They are staring at me in silence, but I can see through their shoelaces. The heels are whispering, "Oh, look, she is in love with those expensive shoes. She doesn't want us anymore, we are old and used." I know they are right, I don't want them anymore. They can't keep my feet warm or help me feel comfy. They can't understand, but it's not about their age or how much they are used, it's about they are close to death and can't take my feet's weight. They worked very well for years, more than what I paid for them.

A pair of shoes are sitting in the middle of store. They look very comfy and nice. I have to try them on. I ask the salesperson to give me a pair my size and sit on a small seat in the store. I take off one of my shoes and feel he looks bad and sick. When I was wearing them, he wasn't that bad. I push him under my seat and wait for the seller. She comes back and tells me they don't have my size. I have been hearing this for years; any pair of shoes I like is not made in my size. I wear my sick shoe and think, *What? My appearance is that bad, you think I can't afford these shoes?* For a moment, that man on the street comes into my head; they couldn't find his size either? How long was he searching for his size? Apparently, shoe companies don't make his and my size.

Suddenly, my old shoes look good. I should probably buy another pair from Walmart; I notice they always have my size. Coming out of the store, I look for another shoe store a few blocks from this one. I stop in front of the store and look inside. There are many women inside, mostly mothers and daughters, and interestingly, the daughters are all trying on expensive shoes and asking their moms if they look good. Any time I am trying to buy a pair of shoes, I am faced with this type of buyer around me; it is like they are trying to rub their relationships, families, and money in my face. I take another look at my shoes. We went through a lot together; traveled, looked for jobs, bought groceries in bad weather, and when we got disappointed with bus rides, walk together, we understood each other. I think it will take a while for my new shoes to understand me. For some reason, those women inside the store make me uninterested in going inside. It is a pair of high heel shoes; I can hear them everywhere. I heard them many times in offices, and in malls they follow me like they want to remind me they put their feet in my shoes when I had a job and money; but something about the noise they make is aggressive and threatening, like they are after revenge from those who are wearing high heels, or have to wear nice shoes for their jobs, or are going to parties and salons. I don't know, it is something about those heels. Somehow, it's like they are trying to show me I am out and it's time that youngsters who can afford to walk in those shoes replace me. I stop in the middle of the mall to let those spy shoes pass, but suddenly I can't hear them anymore. I smile and think, *time flies on, and you will be spied on wearing younger, prettier shoes soon.* I change my path and turn back to see where those shoes are going but they have disappeared. Okay, it's fine now, they left my shoes. We can walk to another store, try not to think about them.

I stop in front of a sporting store. Inside are all types of sneakers for men and women. They are sharp and look like they are ready to run. I walk inside and go straight to the women's shoes. I can walk with them, they are my style, but the price is too high. Most of the customers are teens or in their twenties. I notice the parents are looking at me amazed, like; *what are you doing here? Are you a kid?* I don't know if it is my shoes or my look that makes them judge. In my memory, I search for those times I was in high heels or wearing sporty sneakers to find out what it is about my shoes they are interested in, but I get nothing. I guess I never thought about my shoes' situation till my feet were freezing in the snow. I still have good shoes in my closet, but they are not just suitable for walking and taking public transport. I am saying this to make myself feel better; *Today, I am buying a pair of shoes, and next time I will wear one of my good pairs of shoes when I come to the mall.* In my head again, I can see that man on the street. No, I am not him and never will be. I take a rubber and delete his image from my mind, but he is stocked in some part of my head and as I am faced with those shoes, his image is coming back to me.

I am searching for my size and trying to kick negative thoughts out of my head. I can hear two pairs of shoes talking beside me. At first, I do not look. I sit down to try a pair of sneakers on, but they are making fun of my shoes and don't leave them alone. While my head is lowered to put on the new shoes, I slowly turn my head to my left to where those shoes are talking and look at them. They are two pairs of flat black and old-style shoes; one pair is male, another one is female, but it looks like they were bought at the same time and from one store. Both styles are the same, just with a different gender. Behind them are another brand-new pair of shoes looking beautiful, and it seems like they are all together. In a moment, the pretty pair are off their owner's feet and she is trying an expensive pink sparkly sneakers and those other two pairs are looking and admiring. I want to know why they are talking about my shoes and making my shoes feel bad. They hide under the seat and look sad and annoyed. The two pairs of shoes know each other; one of them is pointing at my shoes under the seat and asking the other one, "What is wrong with them, and why is she trying another pair?" She replies, "Their owner feels young, and at her age thinks she should wear a pair of sneakers like *that*." She points to a costly pair of shoes and both roll their eyes and get back to looking at the pink shoes. I don't know if it is their talking behind my shoes' back or comparing those sparkly shoes with mine that is making all the shoes I try on unfit. It is like I don't deserve anything else except what I have. I just can't sit there anymore; I put my shoes back on and leave. When I am looking around, I think, *Did my shoes ask for money from those pairs of shoes or pay for their replacement? What the hell was that?* Now my shoes started bugging me. I didn't think my shoes were that important a subject. I look down at my shoes and think I should go to the washroom and clean them. I feel bad for my shoes, they have been with me for a long time. I don't know whether the other shoes were being sarcastic when they asked what is wrong with them or were making fun of me, not my shoes. I run to the washroom and after washing my hands, use some paper towel to clean them. They are pleased with this move and try to be thankful, but I am sure they are thinking about that conversation too. Probably, they think, "What? We are good now? Or is this supposed to be funny?" They look at each other and stop talking. I can hear their thoughts. I smile at them; it is okay, we still could walk and talk and listen together.

I do some window shopping around without going inside. Some of those shoes look great, especially those ankle boots. I can buy one pair but I have to prioritize my buying. I walk out of the mall and think, *I'll come back another day when a couple of those shoes are not here.* After five minutes, my clean shoes turn muddy with white spots and I feel some melted snow is getting inside my shoes. I can feel them shaking because of being wet in this weather. I try to speed up my steps to get to the bus station, but it is far from the mall. I don't look at my shoes to see how they are falling apart; I pretend everything is perfectly fine. During these thoughts, I see one old sneaker coming from the opposite side of the road. Without moving my head, I try to guess why he is on his own. Where is his partner? He is coming closer. Interesting; he is single and carrying the weight of a boy's body all alone but looks solid, like he never needed his partner and that's why he lost her. For a second, I look at my shoes; they are stepping fast but are not as strong as that single shoe. The only thing next to that shoe is a crutch, as if he is a tree or plant that needs to lean on something to grow. He must have lost his partner in a war, an accident, or… For a second, my breath is stuck inside my lungs as his owner's face is almost in mine. I guess I was so busy looking at his shoe that I forgot to look where I was going. I move my body quickly out of the way and as I do so, I can see his face; he is a boy, around 15, with one leg and half of his other leg, walking with a cane. His brown hair is falling from his black hat and covering the right side of his face. For a moment, his brown eyes catch my eyes, as if he is asking, "What are you looking at? You never saw a boy with one leg?" I lower my head and almost run to the bus station. I try not to think about him but his look into my eyes was effective and for some reason I forget about my wet, dirty shoes. At least I have two legs and can walk on my feet.

I run to the bus station, and in a few minutes the bus shows up. I jump on the bus and get one of the back seats that is located on a higher level. I take my backpack and put it on the seat beside me. Then I think if any passenger hops on, I will move it. It is full of snow and my hat and jacket are wet too. I push my shoes under the bus heater to make them warm. I don't want to look at them; this way, at least, I can't read their minds or hear their thoughts. I am on the bus for the next twenty minutes; it is warmer and I have a seat. That is all that matters for now.

At the next bus station, I jump off the bus. It is a long walk home; those shoes make it hard to walk. I look around, trying to find another bus to take me closer to my apartment. I see a bus stop sign but there's no sign of any bus. I take down the phone number from the bus sign and call to ask for the bus schedule. A woman puts me on hold. I have no choice except to stay on the line. After one minute, she says there are no buses at this hour. The last bus left two hours ago. I hang up disappointed; my feet are freezing. Other than me, there are just a few people on the street. Others are inside their cars and perhaps their car heaters are keeping them warm, and they are listening to music or chatting with each other. Across the street, I see two girls walking. They are cold too, but not because of their shoes. They look good; I guess they are going to or coming from a party and because they were drinking had to walk or take a bus. I am standing in the bus station desperately, knowing no bus will be showing up. Cold, tired, and still upset by my experiences in the mall, I can hear the sound of a shoe behind me. I don't turn round to see who is coming, but it makes me less insecure if I know someone else is in my situation. Those shoes are not lifting their owner's feet; it sounds like they are pulling themselves. I wait for the shoes to get closer. My eyes follow them while they pass me. They are a pair of sporty grays, like my shoes, they are wet and tired; either their owner is too tired to take full steps, or it is his style to drag his feet. He makes a narrow line of footsteps in the snow behind him, like a passing bicycle. I can see just his back; he is wearing a warm winter jacket without a hat or scarf. It looks like he is used to this weather. He doesn't seem bothered by the snow; he just pulls his legs along with him. He probably lives very close and has come from home to buy a box of cigarettes or a lottery ticket.

I am still debating whether to walk or to see what other options I have. I look at my shoes again; I don't think we can make it. I check the price for taking an Uber; it is not very expensive, by car, it should take 10 minutes, while walking should be around 30 minutes. Okay, I call an Uber. I am freezing under the snow. Where is that car? Everywhere is completely white. Since I am the only one standing under snow, the driver should be able to see me if he is around. I text him my location and wait for another 10 minutes. I call Uber again.

"Where are you?"

He responds he is on his way and hangs up. I can't feel my legs anymore, and my shoes are complaining; "If we had walked, we would be home now; we're not sure we can survive. Where is your driver?" I don't have anything to say; I just watch them disappearing into the snow. The ice is getting to my ankle. I check every car plate passing. I think that if this car doesn't show up, I will have to walk. There is no bus at this hour, and there is no one to help me. After another five minutes, finally I see a car stop in front of me. Thank God, my Uber is here. I get inside, angry and upset.

"Why did it take so long?" I ask.

He is whispering something I don't hear, and I am really not in the mood to listen.

He drops me off in front of my apartment. I really want to see his shoes, but they are hiding beside his seat. When I get to my lobby, I look at my shoes and tell them we survived. One of them says with a sarcastic voice, "This time." I know she is right; next time, neither of us might survive. I run to my suite and once in, take off my shoes. Oh, the insides of them are terrible! There is nothing I can do for them. I take my socks off and throw them in the laundry, change my clothes, and go to bed to make myself warm. I know tomorrow I will go to the mall and this time I will be wearing one of my good pairs of shoes.

It is Sunday. Today, the mall's hours are not the same as on weekdays. I look through my apartment window; the area is covered with snow and ice all over, even the cars stuck inside the parking area. I think, as they have tires instead of shoes, those are probably whining too. At the same time, I see a driver jump into his truck and after a few back and forth on the wheel, the truck is out of the parking area. He could get rid of the snow easily. I should do that too.

I get dressed and go inside my closet, looking at my shoes. I have a nice, girly, sparkly pair of long boots and a few pairs of business shoes. After a few minutes thinking, I pick an ankle boot with a three-centimeter heel. It's waterproof so it should be good for snow and shopping. I know these shoes put pressure on my feet, especially if I need to wait for a long time in the bus station or walk, but I take them. I have to show those other pairs that my shoes are good and I still can afford a good pair. I wear them and try to listen to what they say. I look at them for a few minutes; they are quiet, as if they don't want to say anything to disappoint me or it is their style to be quiet.

I feel taller. I put on my hat and go out of my apartment. I know the mall's business hours are half-day, but whatever; I am not that man lying down on the street, I won't be. I have to keep myself up, it is the only way. Outside is like walking on an island of ice; most people are in their cars and barely anyone is walking. I am trying not to focus on weather; instead, I see how beautiful the trees look under the ice and snow. What a gorgeous view. In some places, I have to change my route or even go from the walkway to the street because of the snow and ice. Some places have been cleaned, but there is a layer of ice all over the walkway. I am very close to the bus station. I wait for green light to cross over; it takes long time. While I am waiting at the intersection, I am covered by dirty melted ice thrown up at me by the tires of cars that are driving off. I step back and try to clean my jacket and look those tires with anger. I lower my head to see how my shoes are doing; they are standing quiet and strong like nothing has happened or to say, *So what, it is just melted ice, not a big deal*. I think I should wear those shoes more often.

Finally, I am at the bus station. It is very cold. I run through the glass doors into the station. There is a paper cup on the bench. I don't want to sit on that bench, it might make my pants dirty. I stand there for a while; just a few passengers come inside. I look at their shoes. What is happening? This time, theirs all look bad compared to mine. It's like they are against me; when my shoes were old, they all looked good; today, they all look old and sick. My shoes try not to look at them. My shoes are cold but strong, they just want to get on the bus. When a bus arrives, I step out of the station to make sure the driver hasn't missed me. It's happened before and I blamed my shoes, but not this time. The bus stops and the middle door opens in front of my face. For some reason, I know that when the first, middle or third bus doors open in my face, it is related to the type of shoes I am wearing. I get on the bus. Those few passengers are hopping on at the last door. I want to sit on the first seat available, but the way the other passengers sit makes it seem as if I am not allowed to sit anywhere, in the same way that I am not allowed to get on the bus using the door I want to. I get to a seat in the middle that is again located at a higher level; I think my shoes deserve to sit here.

This bus is not very busy. My next ride should be interesting, and visiting the mall on a Sunday should create a story. My shoes sitting under my seat say nothing, just observing and waiting for the next bus and of course going to the mall. I try to listen to their inside thoughts. They are quiet and I can't hear what they say. "Okay, we'll see," I say to my shoes. "You can't stay quiet all day, you should say something." And I turn my head to the window. Now that my shoes are saying nothing, I don't want to look at other shoes, not now anyway.

It is a long, silent ride. The bus turns into the bus station and my shoes strongly stand up and get off the bus. I walk to the station to wait for the connecting bus. Suddenly, all shoes around me look small. I am very sure that depending on what shoes I am wearing, other shoes change their appearance. Yesterday, they all were looking down at my shoes but today all the shoes pass conscientiously like they are scared of my shoes or are very much weaker than mine and it is my shoes' responsibility to help them. I look at the shoes along the station and those under the benches; they are expecting something from my shoes and look at them as if my shoes have taken everything they had. I want to know what my shoes have to say. I listen to them, but they say nothing, just stand tall. I think, *Great, today is my day in shopping mall, I don't have to hide my shoes.*

The bus is here and we all get on it. Anywhere my shoes go to find a seat, someone else runs and takes it. I can hear them telling each other, "Don't let her sit, look at her shoes, her shoes are waterproof and she can't feel what we feel." For some reason, I don't feel sorry for them anymore. I think, yesterday my shoes were wet, dirty, and falling apart. No one even tried to listen or talk to them, but today everyone is expecting my boots to jump up and take them out of the ice, dirt, and snow. Look at my shoes; they look okay but they're not as great as those shoes pretend they are. I bought them when they were on sale; I thought they could keep my feet out of the snow, but walking with them is not easy. I feel my back hurting; I am tired and need to sit, but today the bus is full of poor, weak, and needy shoes, and I have to stand to be punished for my shoes' height.

It is a long ride, but finally we are at our destination. Those needy shoes run in front of me, rolling their eyes at my boots as if to say, "You don't belong to us." I wait, letting them all get off the bus first, and then step out. It is freezing cold. I try not to show how cold I am. It takes ten minutes to get inside the mall; it is very crowded. Everywhere are kids' shoes running and playing around. Some weaker shoes are under benches; a few pair of nice shoes are around, but they feel like my shoes. Every pair is staring at them and asking for something. I walk to the closest shoe store. Inside, it is full of expensive, beautiful shoes. I know I won't be buying them, but it feels good going inside and pretending you can afford them. For some reason the other shoes talking behind my shoes' back. It makes me try on some expensive pairs. I think, *Ha, now I am trying this on and you can be jealous all day*. I take off one of my shoes as soon as I want to try a pair of tall, gorgeous boots. It's like a bomb is exploding in the store. Those shoes are all over the store changing, walking, talking and they are very loud. I am very sure they do this on purpose to distract and annoy me. It's like I am stealing their money to buy a new pair of shoes. A salesperson comes to me and asks if the boots are okay or if I need another size. I can see my shoes are smiling in the corner, like the three of us know they are not treating me the same as before. I am the same person I was yesterday; she is treating my shoes, not me. I thank her and think, *I am not buying this if you must know*. After a few tries, I leave and notice that other pairs are coming after me. I try to step faster but I can't get rid of them, they are everywhere; in the food court, on every floor and in the stores. I want to see my shoes say something, anything, tell me they know how I feel, or have sympathy for me, or at least tell me I am wrong; but they are too strong to complain or say something. I go to the food court, find a table and sit. I feel lonely. My shoes say nothing, but I can see all the other shoes are talking. A bunch of small, colorful shoes are running. I really don't want be part of this show; it seems they all are doing this on purpose, pointing at me and saying, "Your shoes are tall and strong but lonely we all are together, playing, gossiping, and making fun of your shoes."

I wish my shoes could tell me they feel hungry. This way, we could go to one of the stores without them thinking I'm putting pressure on them and order something. I have to eat, anyway. Looking around, I find a queue for fried chicken; most of the shoes in this queue seem to be carrying a lot of weight and are large-sized. Okay, I am joining this line, I can pretend I am big too, who cares? I am wearing good shoes and today I can afford anything I want. I feel like a kid in a wonderland who can pick and buy anything she wants because it is her birthday. I get my food tray to take back to my seat, but it's the same scenario; that couple of pairs of shoes run to every table I am targeting, and a bunch of noisy kids' shoes are with them. I don't know whether it is my shoes' silence or my anger at how people can change color and make judgments based on what I am wearing that makes me eat my food as fast as I can and run to the next expensive shoe store.

In this store, customers are really buying shoes. There are pairs of big sneakers; they look comfy, warm, and expensive. This is what I want, but their tag price means I would need a large amount of money. There is one pair of ankle sneakers I particularly like that has everything I need; they are comfy, stylish, sparkly, and warm. I take one of them, turn it and look at the price on the bottom, then lower my head to my boots to see what they say. They just stare at me and don't say a word, but I know them; they don't mind if I buy these. I can even feel they are supporting me. I put shoe on the tray and go sit on the small bench down the store. I need to do some calculations in my head. If I buy this pair, I can wear them all cold season long and even after, but spending that much money might lead me to be short of money to pay bills. I stand up to leave, but my shoes get heavy like they want me to buy this pair. The same way they don't say a word, I don't say a word and leave and take them with me. I really want to tell them; *Today I am wearing you, but tomorrow I have to get back to my old shoes for jumping on the bus and running after public transport in snow; I have to survive*. But the way they look at me is like they know and ask; *Don't say it, just don't.*

I spend four hours in mall looking around for a good pair of shoes at a fair price. It is close to 6 p.m., and as it is Sunday, the mall will be closed soon. I have tried many shoes; some of them did not fit, some were not my size, and some fit beautifully, but I didn't buy them because something about them made me unwilling to buy, it might have been my shoes I am wearing. I think; *What if I buy another expensive boots and they don't talk to me either? What if they can't understand me and are just proud of their height but just look good and pricey and don't even feel hungry when I do? What if they don't even feel the pain in my feet, when their style is more important than being comfy?* I am going home. No, today I am not buying anything. I ask myself, *Did my shoes hear what I said?* They don't talk, anyway; apparently they prefer to stay in the closet and rub their look and cost in other pairs of shoes' faces. Deep down, I wish they could hear my thoughts; this way, next time they might say something or at least feel sympathy. It is like I am taking revenge on all the shoe stores that yesterday were making fun of me and today are talking behind my shoes, which say nothing.

Okay, now I feel much better. I walk out of the mall, check the time on my cell phone and the bus schedule to make sure I'll be able to get the next one. I think my shoes have heard my thoughts, because several times they try to slip on the ice and make me fall, but I successfully catch my bus and sit on a seat on the higher level. For a minute, I check others' shoes; they are all jealous and think they deserve those shoes or my shoes owe them something. Whatever; tomorrow is another day, but I am not going to be jealous of other shoes. I can pick any pair I wish; and those thoughts make me happy, and I smile.

In my apartment, I take off my shoes, clean them, and put them back inside the closet. It is like I am telling them, *Stay here, think about what you did today and laugh*. I still need a pair of shoes; my old shoes look awful. While I am having my dinner, I think about where I should go to shop, but tomorrow is a workday and I need my business shoes. I have noticed that in the office some girls are wearing shiny high heels while others stick with comfy shoes. I do not wear my sneakers in the office either; I have to wear my safety shoes for working outside, my three-centimeter black shoes or my comfy sandals. Either way, it won't be my leather boots or my old shoes. Before going to bed, I go back and look at my old shoes. We have a good conversation; they understand if I need to wear a different pair and wish me luck.

In the morning, I pick my three-centimeter black shoes; they look good and are businessy and fit with my dress very well. They tell me, in business you should look good and, if necessary, you can walk too. However, these shoes don't have high heels and they look comfy, but really, they are not; my toes are already in pain, but this is business, and in the office we don't argue too much. I call a cab because in this weather it is impossible to walk in these shoes; I need a taxi to the subway station; my shoes agree with me. We sit in the back of the taxi and wait for our destination. They are talking about other shoes in the office – those gorgeous purple shoes, those stylish white shoes – and as soon as they got to the point of mentioning shiny brown shoes, suddenly I am interested. There's something about those shoes, I don't know what, that makes me curious. I try to listen carefully to see what my shoes are saying about them. One of my shoes tells the owner of the brown shoes is hiding something, the other one thinks he is handsome, and they have a conversation about how to deal with those shoes if they show up in a meeting today. For a moment, the thought of all those shoes under the meeting room table, talking and evaluating each other, comes into my head. Suddenly, I think, *OMG, they all know what we say and how we feel about each other; I hope they stay quiet and do not step on each other by accident* – and suddenly I laugh out loud. The driver looks through the mirror to see why I am laughing. I pretend it wasn't me and think, *You must be crazy, I am not talking to my shoes*; then I can hear myself laughing inside.

The taxi drops me off in the subway bus station, a short walk to the subway. My legs are freezing but I'm used to it. It's what I have been doing for years every day. I swipe my card and enter the subway. As I wait for the train, it is busy, and I can see many shoes around me. In a minute, the train is here, and I can hop on it. I am amazed how fast the other shoes run and compete against each other to take seats; in 30 seconds all the seats are occupied by passengers. I walk along the aisle of the train to find a seat in another side, and I think that designers of trains should consider how we are supposed to squeeze into the middle seat of a set of three seats.

I try to listen to a group of engineers and manufacturers. Their shoes are of two types; a stylish, strapless female pair and an expensive black male pair. They monitor details all over the train, checking passengers' shoes and how they are sitting or walking, or even how every shoe enters the train or how they react to the train moving or stopping, and how exhausted they get when standing for a long time or squeezing themselves into an uncomfortable seat. They are in a long narrow corridor and there is not enough room available; it needs to be fixed. Those strapless shoes talk to each other without letting the black shoes hear. "OMG, do we need to sit here for at least half an hour?" "No way, these feet inside my shoes will be killed by every pair of shoes that's passing or stepping on them. I have to hide under the seat, but there's not enough room there. I can't be replaced with another pair of closed-toe shoes; besides, in this day and age, I am top fashion…" And she looks at her partner, rolling her eyes. When she wants to talk to the black male shoes, she knows they don't understand and thinks, *So what? If they step on me, I can clean myself when I get to the destination; they are not hurting my feet. If you are worried about your feet, use a closed shoe, not a pair of sandals without socks.* I can see this female pair are exploding with anger, but they are working together and there is no room for fighting. I get back to the main part of the train, and finally I find a seat in a set of two seats in the front row, opposite a set of three seats, and take one by the window. My shoes are happy; they shouldn't have to carry my weight for at least the next hour.

I hope my side-seat gets occupied by someone who don't smash me into the window. My head is down, and I am just looking at shoes. A pair of girly shoes are sitting beside mine. I think, *Thank God, we both have some room on these tiny seats*, but at this moment a big pair of sneakers, I guess they are size 13 to 14, caught my eyes. Interesting; they are not moving. It seems their owner already has a seat, but I don't understand why it looks like they are in the aisle of the train. Slowly, I move my eyes from those big shoes to their owner, and when I get to his head, I am shocked to find his head is in front of me. How come his shoes are in the middle of the train? It takes 10 to 15 seconds for me to realize he is sitting on the set of three seats across from my seat; that's why I can see his head in front of me. But the seats are too tiny for him; he is almost lying down on the seats, and that means his legs and shoes are almost in the aisle of the train, and it's clear that neither I nor that girl next can get out of our seats unless he moves. I try to hold my knees closer to my body to be sure they do not touch the side of his body that is opposite my seat, but it is impossible. I put my bag between his body and my knees. This is a very uncomfortable seating arrangement, but as long as I am on window seat at least no one will step on my shoes, and they are safe. I look at the other girl's shoes. They are blue and orange with heels and look expensive, and her skirt is covering part of her legs, but she is in the same situation as me and is trying very hard to hold her shoes and body far from this other passenger's touch. Because of this, she is almost leaning on me, and her blond hair is on my shoulder.

She moves a lot. I try to stay in my seat and pretend I am okay, but I can't breathe; my shoes are screaming, *Get us out of here!* I jump out of my seat at the next station and run to the door. While the passengers are getting off the train and everyone expects me to step out, I hold onto a pole by the door and take a breath. My feet are killing me; those business shoes are definitely not made for standing on the train or tucking your feet tight behind the seat to get away from other shoes. My shoes tell me we have already had a long day, and this is starting to make them tired. I just look at them; I have nothing to say. I know how they feel but there is no other option. I want to yell at them, "Be quiet!" but when they are right, they are right.

There are at least six or seven stations to my destination. For a moment, I wish I had my old pair of shoes on my feet, but I know they are not for business. Tomorrow I will have to change my shoes for another pair, they might be better. While I am thinking, a sudden stop makes all the passengers standing in the aisle of the train almost stack on top of each other, and some gray boots crush my left shoe. I can hear she is whining and is in pain, but what can we do? We are all climbing on top of each other, and everyone tries to get back to their place. In this mess, I notice a woman, around 65, who was pushed. It almost looks as if she is sleeping on the train floor. No one really cares; the others who are standing are suffering as much as her, and those who are sitting probably found a seat after a long waiting period or are squeezing themselves into the aisle. I try to move to the corner, then see that woman changes her position from sleeping to sitting on the floor. My shoes are not going to sit, they are standing and keeping my feet ready; this is what I say to myself.

After a long ride, I am finally at my destination. On the bright side, there is no need to walk out of the station; to get to my office, I can take the underground walkway. In the office, there are shoes everywhere; an important meeting is happening, and the shoes are running from this side to that side and making too much noise; the sound goes straight into my ears like a killing whistle. I go to my office and get ready for the meeting. In 15 minutes, we are all sitting around the table. No one is talking, there is no noise except for pages turning, and all the shoes are quiet. It is like they are having a party under the table; I really want to drop something and use this excuse to look at the attendees' shoes, but that sounds very lame. I think, *At least the meeting is two hours, and I have time*. After five minutes, the secretary starts reading the agenda and people start to talk. Based on what they are saying, I try to guess what shoes they are wearing. Some of them must be wearing safety shoes; their talk shows they are practical, not office people. It's like someone has grabbed them and they have been seated here by force. Some of them are surely wearing high-class shoes; these are mostly those who are speaking, listening and giving orders. Some of employees are probably wearing either high heels or a mid-style pair of shoes; they are not talking too much, As a matter of fact, they don't really seem to be in this meeting and are just counting down to when they can get out of the room and go for lunch. As I look around, just two people are interesting. One says nothing but looks like he can read everyone's mind; he looks at everybody while they are speaking and makes notes, no more than a few words at a time. I am sure no one except him would know what he is writing or what the purpose is of those notes, even if they spent hours reading them. Another one's head is down. He does not look at anyone; it is like he doesn't want to judge anyone based on their shirts or suits. But now and then he will say something that no one can respond to or comment on; his word is final. I think about what these two men's shoes look like. They must be shiny brown shoes. I don't know why I think that. I try to find a related subject that could help me know why those brown shoes mean something, but nothing comes to my mind, except that anytime I have noticed an impressive person speaking, walking, or even shaking hands, they were wearing brown shoes. A girl with a very nice-looking dress who is sitting beside me tries to stand up to pass some reports. She knocks my pen off the table; it is my moment. She tries to apologize but I jump down to retrieve it and for 30 seconds can look all the shoes under the table. I can see those brown shoes. One of the pairs is shiny; it's very stylish, as if made from a special fabric, one is flat. The other is an ankle boot. They both look wonderful, and I have no doubt they belong to those two men I guessed. They are the first who leave the meeting. It means the meeting is over; another final statement. The safety shoes almost run out of the room and even compete against each other to escape; they belong to the outside world. The rest of the shoes, including my own, are still in room and try to have a friendly or businessy chat. We belong to the middle-class business world; our words are not final unless we get approval. We are not outdoor persons either; we like to stay inside and only be outside when the situation demands it. Our shoes are not expensive; however, some of them are very stylish. My shoes feel comfortable among this type of shoes; they think these are not as smart as those brown shoes or as practical as the safety shoes. After a few minutes standing, I again sit on one of the seats close to the door, making room for those who want to leave behind my seat. My shoes are under the table; they can talk about their ideas freely, but as long as they are in this environment, I can see some of the stylish shoes looking at each other, and sometimes it gets tense. My shoes think these shoes might step on each other and try to stay away from them.

After business hours, my shoes run out of the office. They have a long way to get home, and this time it is better; they can catch a train where the seats are not opposite others. Finally, we are home. I take the shoes off and with bare feet walk all over my apartment. It feels great; no limitation, free and comfy. I think that's why I like my apartment. My old shoes are sitting beside my business shoes. I take them and put in a shoe box; I try not to make them feel bad. I walk all over my apartment without shoes on for at least 10 minutes, then I see my inside sandals are staring at me as if they are saying, *What is wrong with you? We are sitting right here in front of you.* I get them. They are comfy and my feet can breathe. I walk with them on to my closet and look at my shoes that are sitting on the open shoe boxes. Tomorrow, I will be wearing… My eyes turnaround; I look at all the boxes and pick an open ankle-boot with a five-centimeter heel. They look good, however; they are stylish, but I know they would never step on other shoes. It is the middle of winter, but by taking a taxi and the subway I won't have to walk outside. I will be okay. In a minute, they are replaced in the shoe box by the shoes I took off at the front door, and they are ready to be worn.

At the office, I notice that everyone is looking at my shoes. I know they look good; although they have high heels, are comfy. Besides, I have to go with those shoes to a management meeting. In half an hour, my shoes and I are in the meeting, they give me confidence. I know they do their best to be fashionable, comfy, and supportive. I take a seat close to the door; for some reason, I like seats close to doors, because any time I feel uncomfortable or bored, I can get out of the office quickly. Shoes are coming in one after another; I am glad my shoes are on the same level as these shoes. They all look good. There are female shoes with and without heels, stylish and clean; even if they were bought with a credit card, the owner must have very good credit. Today, I can't see those brown shoes. When they are in any meeting, every shoe is following their steps and waiting to see what they ask or want, but today all the shoes are under the table. Some of them are sitting like they are shoe goddesses and expect all eyes to be on them; some are strong and bossy, and some are relaxed. During the meeting, I can feel the shoes are talking under the table, but their talking is different this time; they are talking about news, global events, and management styles. I can't see whether my shoes be bored; based on what they say, it seems they are on the same level or one step up or down. They know what their place is and don't want to be replaced with another pair. I am glad about my choice; there wasn't a better option for this meeting, and inside my head I am happy I got a pedicure. Unlike at some meetings, my shoes are not disappointed or tired, they do not pressure my feet and after half-time they are very relaxed and have found many friends who can have a good conversation. On my way back home on the train, they are criticized by other shoes as if they are telling them, "Aren't you cold?" I can hear they are gossiping; "Look at them! With this ice, how can they take steps? What show-offs, look at their nail polish." I try not to look at those shoes, I am scared they may step on my shoes on purpose and crush my feet. My head is up as I stand in the aisle of the train and pray to find a seat where I can hide my shoes. I can see several seats unoccupied, but I can hear those who are already sitting say, "Don't even think about it, you don't belong with us. Why are you not taking a taxi with your bossy shoes?" And calling the other shoes on the train. There is a storm inside the train; they are talking aloud, making fun of my shoes, pushing me from this side to that. My shoes are trying very hard to keep their balance and not fall. I ask my shoes to stay calm and that we will get off the train soon, but they are suffering on their high heels, and in this cold environment they are shaking. I think, *What is wrong with these people? You are the same people who didn't let me sit in the station when my shoes were come apart, then were around me admiringly when I was wearing my silent shoes, and now this?* At this moment, I hear an inside scream that is coming from my shoes. They are crushed under an ugly big pair of shoes; yes, he stepped on my shoes and my feet are now muddy and scratched. I try to see what these shoes look like; their shoelaces are not in the right holes, they are tied almost halfway, they are full of mud and dirt as if they have not been cleaned for long time. Interesting, they are standing very close to a female pair similar to them and they are talking very happily with each other. It seems like that female pair is jubilant with him for stepping on my feet, or perhaps she even asked him to do that. My shoes are injured, annoyed and insulted; they are looking at me like I have taken them to a party without an invitation. They are right. I knew it might happen. I have been taking this train long enough to know how they would react. They should be angry with me; all the other shoes are together, and we are alone. I try to escape from those looks to another part of the train, but it is all the same. I walk to the end of the train; at least I am close to the door and can jump out if those looks don't get better. My feet hurt and this pain is coming up into my legs and head. I tell my shoes, "Hang on, we're going home."

It is another evening walking around my apartment with bare feet, and nothing can take this moment from me. It is my home I can walk anywhere with anything I like, or with nothing at all. I laugh out loud; it's like I am trying to shoot all my anger out of my body. I even dance for a few minutes without wearing my shoes. I feel much better now. I put this pair of shoes in their shoe box too. Tomorrow, I am trying another pair. I look at all of them; something inside me is telling me, *Pick your safety shoes*. Tomorrow you will spend time outside; you will have a day full of adventure. I take them out and leave them in front of my apartment door. They look strong. I know that even if someone tries to step on them, they won't break or even scratch. I feel confident tomorrow will be a good day. I go to bed to wake up early for a new day.

I can't believe how easy it is walking in these shoes. I can jump or even kick a rock and I don't feel anything. I even wonder whether I can take a bus instead of the taxi to get to the subway, though I have to get to work on time. I get into the taxi; my shoes are sitting within a small distance of the seat. I look at them; they are telling me, "Today no one can bother you, we are here and can smash those who are stepping on you and us." I don't know if it is our conversation or replacing my usual skirt with a pair of jeans that makes me feel as if I am able to do anything. In my head, I think I can lift up a big barrier or jump over it. I am laughing again, and the taxi driver is looking at me in his mirror, but I really don't care if he thinks I am crazy. I tell the driver with my inside voice, *Today I am wearing my safety shoes, you better be careful who you are talking to*, and I laugh.

On the train, it's another story. There are shoes all over the place. The same gossip and talking, targeting a pair of shoes to humiliate them, talking behind their back, or stepping on them. I am standing in the aisle of the train. Today, with these shoes and pants, I am not concerned about finding a seat. I think that if someone steps on my feet, I can kick his leg. This way, I can get revenge for my other shoes, but I know I won't do it. In a few minutes, the train is full, and I can barely breathe. This time, my shoes are safe, but I get hit in my face, head, and hands. It makes me want to kick these people's legs, but that's not me, I can't be like them. That's why I can try any shoes I want. I try to pull myself into the corner; at least here I am protected on one side of my body, and even if my body comes into contact with a sitting passenger, at least it is not pressed.

Close to my station, while I am trying to move between two rows of passengers, my shoes touch a pair of greenish shoes and suddenly the owner is screaming like hell. I want to say sorry, but my voice sticks inside my mouth. I look at her shoes to see what I have done, but really nothing happened. My words are in my mouth, but they are holding my teeth tightly closed; they don't want to come out and tell this woman they are sorry. What should they do? These are the same people and the same shoes that bug my feet every day. I am trying to push words out of my mouth but when I see every eye on the train staring at me and the passengers rolling their eyes, I am not willing to say anything. I think, *Whatever; so what if it was my feet, you were all laughing when this happened. Besides, I barely touched those ugly feet.* I can hear my teeth and words are having a party, laughing and dancing; they are telling each other, "Today is our day." My shoes are looking at me. They are not asking me to do or say anything; they know what I am going through. They are just there to protect me.

Finally, I get off the train and walk to the office. I know that, unlike elsewhere, my shoes are not very popular within the office, especially if those high-style shoes see them. I try to stay away from those; I know my safety shoes are not interested in touching them. I won't be in the office for very long. My shoes will go outside with the other safety shoes, and they will have a great day.

After a few hours, all my shoes' friends are here, and we take two cars to go outside. It is like these shoes are in a different world. My shoes feel safe and know they won't be stepped on. With these shoes, I can go anywhere, no matter if it is full of metal, concrete, or mud. They are made for this type of environment. We have an adventurous day, my shoes jumping from this side to that side, and I know I am protected.

This was a long day, and finally I am home wearing my sandals. Unlike other days, my feet don't feel tired. I wish I could wear these shoes forever, but I replace them with another pair of shoes. I put them in my top-row shoe box to make sure I can see them anytime I want. The other pair are long boots with a sharp heel. You don't know where you should wear them; they are suitable for any environment and at the same time could be inappropriate. They are tall and look good with a skirt. According to the news, tomorrow will be a rainy day, so I can wear them. I think I don't wear them more often because I was keeping them for a rainy day, and I laugh.

It is another day on the subway. This time, as I guessed, the reactions are different. Some think I am okay today, and that perhaps I finally belong to this society; some still doubt I can be part of their world, and the rest think I am a spoiled rich girl who even in this weather is wearing a skirt with long boots. I try to listen to my shoes to see how they feel; they have mixed feelings too. They push me to a seat between two rows of seats which all have two seats and make me sit on the first one. This way they can watch other shoes and be seen. It is a very tight row; my knee is touching the seat in front. I think I must have gained some weight; how come this seat seems so small to me? Without turning my head, I try to see what the person beside me is wearing. They are a pair of boots, without heels, that are longer than ankle-length and shorter than my boots. Inside they have some type of fur. It looks very warm, but they are wet. My shoes are happy to see they would be safe from water on the street and are telling each other, "Look, they are not good for this weather." For a moment, I can hear that even my shoes are evaluating other shoes and I think it must be part of shoes' nature. At least they don't think they do not belong to society. At this moment, someone passing pushes my boots so hard that I think I may fall off my seat. This seat is small, and half of my body is out of it, but still he could have passed without touching me. I am trying to figure out if he was doing it on purpose or it was an accident when I am hit with another one and another one and another one. Suddenly, my shoes and I both are angry. I pull my shoes inside and look at the passenger sitting beside me to see if she at least is trying to be more considerate. But no, she thinks it is her seat and the other passengers that belong to this train, not me. The left side of my leg hurts. After a calculation in my head, it seems that the distance between seat rows is enough for the biggest person to pass without touching, so they are doing this on purpose? I remember how yesterday my safety shoes touched those green shoes and that was an emergency, while today no one thinks it's not okay. I think, *It is not over; I will wear those safety shoes again and then kick your boots*. For some reason, my anger changes to a smile, and I know this smile is killing them. My shoes are sitting under my seat and say, "Ha, they were not expecting this; at least we can manage to smile," and we all smile.

At my destination, I get off the train. My shoes are tall and look good. We walk to the office; others barely notice my shoes. I am happy. This way they are not judging me or my shoes. It is a normal day, walking around with my boots.

When I am in my office, without lifting my head, I just watch the shoes that are passing outside my station. Most of them are clean and professional; some of them look old but clean. During this time, I glance at a few pairs of shoes that are not pleasant; it's like they are saying, "We don't care about this job or you." It is extraordinary; I am sure they have a reason for that. I remember when I was wearing my old shoes how other shoes were talking behind their back. I listen to my shoes to see what they have to say. They have a long conversation about how they will someday turn into those shoes and look old and careless, but they don't realize that this appearance is from being in a bad environment for a long time, or that these are the type of shoes that don't care about anything and believe everyone should accept them. I say nothing, just sitting there and listening to all the shoes that are passing.

It is another day after work, and I am dancing in my homey sandals. It feels really good that nothing can take this moment away from me, being free without judgment or uncomfortable shoes that bother my feet. I can even take off my sandals and walk anywhere with my bare feet.

I lie down on my coach, put my bare feet on the armrest, and feel all my tiredness is gone. I think what type of shoes I should wear at the weekend, searching in my memory to find a pair of shoes suitable for this icy weather. It takes hours; finally, I decide to go shoe shopping again on Friday, and I laugh loudly.

Friday is here. Thank God it is Casual Friday, and I am wearing my sports shoes. They are light; it's like you are not wearing anything. They run ahead of me, taking my body along with them. I know they were bored inside, but the outside is not very welcoming for their bright color. They used to run and do exercise inside. They are not the type of shoes to be fans of icy weather, but we will be in the mall soon. I walk to the mall; I feel much better here and go straight to the shoe store that I know. Look at them, they are sitting on the aisles with different colors and styles. You can hear that some of them are very proud of themselves and are looking to see who deserves to take them home; some are casually relaxed, they don't mind if they are taken to any home; some are sitting on top of the shelves and think that not everyone can touch them. Some of the shoes are on the floor; it is clear they are tired of being tried on and no one liked them, or they did not fit. My sporty shoes are almost flying from this side to that side, looking and talking to other shoes. I see some shoes are rolling their eyes and don't want to have a conversation with them, but in the sports aisle, they seem to be nicer, probably because they learned to be part of a team and are very open to new shoes. While my shoes are chatting, I think, *Why do they like my shoes? Because they look good? Do they treat every pair of shoes like that, or do they know how expensive my shoes are?* But I don't share my thoughts with my shoes, I am glad they are happy and have found some friends. I try a few shoes in this aisle and then go to another side, trying on some shoes that are somewhere between high-class and sporty shoes. They fit and look good, but for some reason they are not the shoes I want today. I need a pair of shoes to wear on the weekend, but I still don't know where I am going or what my plans are. I change stores, going from this side of the mall to that side and trying on many shoes. Some of them are perfect, and I think I have to save up some money and come back for them. Some do not fit and scratch my feet, while some of them are not made for me at all. I tried one pair that has sky-high heels, around 10 to 12 centimeters. I almost lost my balance, then I noticed others staring at me. Walking in those shoes was like driving up a hill when your brake is not working; all my body weight and pressure was on my toes, and I wondered whether the people who wear these really suffer. Interestingly, while I was there, I noticed some customers tried them on and walked like everything was perfect. I laughed inside and told myself, "They are not me at all. Let's get out of here." My shoes and I ran away out of the store.

I spend hours in the mall, getting tired and hungry. It is Friday night, and I could be doing something better than shoe shopping, or at least could be eating my dinner in my sandals. Still, I have one hour to closing time. First, I need to eat. The food court is located in front of one of the shoe stores. I sit on the first seat and think, *Thank God I am not wearing my silent boots*. My sporty shoes are jumping up and down and trying to pick something to eat, but their style is not fast-foody; they prefer something lighter. I don't mind; they are my shoes, and they can pick whatever they want. I am flexible and can eat anything from fried meat to a salad. We get some Japanese food and take a little rest. During my dinner, I suddenly know what I am going to do for the weekend, but I'm not going to tell my shoes. First, I will take them to the shoe store to buy a pair of shoes that are suitable for this weekend, and then they will know what the plan is. I feel like a Lieutenant who discovers who the murderer is but doesn't tell anyone till the time is right. This thought deserves a big smile.

I run to the store I think it should have what I am looking for. There are all types of products here. This store does not specialize in shoes; you can find anything from furniture to tools here, and it has a section with shoes sitting on shelves. My shoes are interested to know what is going on and why I am here. They were expecting a shoe store; they jump over each other, trying to see what I am looking for. In the middle of the rows of shelves, I find those shoes that are suitable for my weekend. They are beautiful; some of them sit in pink, blue, white, and colorful styles on top of the shelves; some, on the lower levels, are strong, black, gray, and dark blue. My shoes are happy now. They know what I am going to do, and they like it. I examine these new shoes one by one because I really don't know which will be best for what I want to do. They all have something in common; they are all good on ice and they all have a sharp blade. The only difference is between blades; some are very sharp, some are a little thinner. I sit on a bench down the aisle and try to read the specifications written on some of their boxes. A salesperson comes to me and asks what I am looking for. He can tell from my look I am very new to this type of shoes and don't know how risky they could be. He looks at my sneakers. I think, *Good, at least he thinks I am a sporty person.* I can see my shoes are laughing but I prefer to ignore them. I tell the salesperson I am trying to start a new adventure and I am looking for something sharp that can stay on the ice and still be in my style. He explains that there are two types; one is good for running and playing on ice, which not everyone can do, while the other type is for dancing on ice. I thank him and pray he leaves soon so I can find a pair I like. In a few minutes, he gives up on me and leaves and I search on the shelves. I like these; we could have an exciting weekend together. Can they cut the ice? I think, *How am I supposed to stay on this thin blade?* I am searching and suddenly I see my shoes; they are sitting on top, beautiful, strong and interested. I check they are the right size. I try them on. They are a little bit pricey, but whatever, I want them. I put them in their box, hold it under my arm and take them to the cashier's desk, and we are going home to get ready for the weekend.

On the Saturday morning, I am waking up excited. These are my new shoes, and I want to see what they can do. It is impossible to wear them before getting to the ice rink. I replace my sporty shoes with my old shoes. Surprisingly, they are still very comfy, I take my new shoes with me to an ice rink close to my home. It is freezing and my old shoes are almost passing out. I run to the changing room; here it is warm, but I am not sure I can stay outside too long. I wear my new shoes; they look great. I tie the shoelaces to make sure I am not hurting my legs on ice. I look at my shoes and whisper, *I am taking a risk by wearing you; don't be a stranger, help me to learn how to stay on the ice the way you know*. They look at each other and I see a mysterious smile on them. I try to stand and walk to the rink and think, *So far so good.* I stop beside the rink curb to watch how other shoes are doing. It is amazing; some of them move like they have lived on the ice forever; some are dancing and some of them are beginners like my shoes. I want to join them. I put one of my shoes on the ice, and suddenly, I am lying down on the ice in the middle of the rink. It is freezing and my leg hurts. Wow, this can't be good; while I am sitting on the ice, some kids' shoes are playing around me. I am very sure they are not supposed to be that close to someone sitting on the ice, whose shoes are clearly still beginners. Standing on the ice is hard, but I am doing it anyway. I slowly go to the curb, which is the border between the ice and the outside, but it doesn't give you any options; you are either that side or this side. My shoes are not bothering; they are standing on the ice with their blade and are carrying my weight. I bend my knees to prevent myself falling again. Those kids' shoes and bunch of younger shoes in their teenage years are trying very hard to show off and are around me all the time. There is not any room for me to try. I take off my shoes and go outside and sit on the bench, which is like sitting in the fire. I wait for a while and see some kids are leaving. I think, *Next time we should come back at night when they are sleep.* My shoes are excited, they want to go on the ice and play. It is very cold, and I think if I don't go back to the rink in the next half hour, there will be an ice statue here instead of me. I go back to the rink and when I am taking some steps and my shoes think we are improving again, kids' shoes and teen couples are around us, cutting in our way and maneuvering on ice. My shoes tell me, "It doesn't matter, they are the same people; no matter what type of shoes you are wearing, you always have problems. We are here to help you, and not everyone can stand on ice." I feel much better. They encourage me to try over and over. In 10 minutes, I am sweating like I am in plus 20-degree weather. It is amazing how my shoes are playing on the ice. They run, walk, and step on ice, but there is no sign of cutting; it is as if they just scratch the ice to show what they can do but won't hurt it. At the same time, those blades are protecting the beauty of the shoes. They are not touching the ice, they sit on top of their blades, and they are protected from dirt and bad weather. After 15 minutes, my heart is beating twice as fast from my exertions; I think this needs too much hard work, at this time it starts snowing. My shoes, now under snow, are pushing me to be better on the ice, to take risks, and not to be afraid of younger shoes. We are doing well, but for my first try I've spent enough time. We leave the rink and walk to the changing room. I take the shoes off, put them in a plastic cover, and put my comfy shoes back on. I can't tell which one is better, my beautiful shoes with the strong blade or my comfy shoes, but either way, I have to run to some place warm. I am not really an outside person in this weather, but we had fun, and I am glad to have bought them. In my apartment, I put them back in their box, take off my old shoes and jump around in my bare feet. OMG, nowhere is like home.

Today, I don't feel like going out. It's cold and there is still snow on the ground; but I can't stay in my apartment all day, it makes me feel useless. After lunch, I take my headphones and put some music on and go to the lobby. I like it here; I can watch snow from every glass wall. I listen to the music and watch the snow. Suddenly I can hear something like whistling on and off. I do not turn my head but slowly turn my eyes to watch which shoes are coming. First is a pair of small pink and white shoes; it must belong to a baby around one year old. They are followed by a pair of flat black shoes and a pair of men's sandals. I think, *Oh, someone else is wearing sandals*. I look at my flip flops; they are lying down on the ground like nothing can take their comfort from them ever and they are happy and light.

I change my position to watch those baby shoes. In every step they are taking, a sound like whistling is coming out of them and they are laughing and are happy. I think how a kid's world is different from adults, those noises are really bothering me, and she is laughing and enjoying as if nothing more enjoyable exists in this world. Those pinky shoes take a few steps and get in each other's way, then the child falls down, and it happens over and over. Those shoes are trying again, like nothing can stop them from getting to the lobby door. With every fall, those black pairs of shoes are following her, laughing and running to help them stand again. What a strange world. If adult shoes fall, is there anyone running to help them? Are any pair of shoes there to encourage them to stand up and walk again? Does any pair of shoes get happy and excited from their efforts and trying? I wish I had an answer to my questions, but this no and no and no is bothering me. My shoes are not with me, they are relaxing watching other shoes and prefer not to listen to my inside whining. While I am thinking, I lose track of those pinky shoes; where are they? I do not turn my head up, just my eyes all over the lobby. They are not here, but I can see those pairs of shoes that were following them. There is no other option, I have to find them. I raise my head; I can see they are hanging between the floor and a woman's head; it must be those flat black shoes that are hugging those baby shoes. The way she hugs those shoes is like they climbed to the top of the Himalayas, they are all happy and celebrating the shoes falling down over and over. It is amazing how we change during our life from those who cheer for a baby's shoes, to use our shoes to compete and then we gradually get tired and give up on shoes. Is it because there is no one cheering for older shoes? Or because no one is there for those failing shoes when they fall ? Or are the shoes simply too busy to care? Whatever, when I see my flip flops are relaxed and sitting under my chair, I try not to think about why, when or how.

In the afternoon, I go to my shoe boxes in my closet to find another pair of shoes. While I am searching, my eyes catch a pair of dark-blue, man-sized plastic slippers. These are definitely not mine; they are at least two sizes bigger. I wonder why they are made of plastic. Probably because they are very flexible and waterproof. Suddenly, I remember many pairs of white plastic slippers. I saw them in hospital; they were everywhere. Most of them couldn't walk properly, some were pulling their owners' legs, some of them were torn. In my memory, I try to turn my eyes from the owners' toes to their heads. I can see their white hairs and the wrinkles on their faces; this part of hospital must belong to the elderly. They look tired, and their eyes have no sense of excitement or curiosity; it is like they are waiting for their due dates. I follow one of them into the hallway. She is carrying a metal shaft that holds a pack of medication. No one is there to support her or be there for her. She is wearing a gray gown that is open at the back and she has no concerns about how she looks or what others think about her. I can hear her shoes, they are saying, "We should find another owner, she won't be with us too long." I can see in this old woman's face that she can hear this too. There's no emotion in her face; it's like she probably left all her emotion and excitement for her kids, or relatives, and now she is alone in hospital. She is pulling her shoes slowly and goes into a room. I try to follow her, but I lost my shoes in this big hospital, I can't find them, and she almost disappears in front of my eyes. I think, *I don't need my shoes, I can follow her with my bare feet.* I run after her to try to see where she went. Just when I am about to give up, I see a small part of her gray gown with some prints of flowers as it is entering a room down the hall. I walk faster and hope nothing on the hospital floor will cut my feet. I stop close to the room to make sure I am not seen. There are two beds inside. One of them is empty; the woman climbs onto the other bed with difficulty. My feet are running in front of me to make me go inside and help her, but we don't. I don't know if she can see me; it is like she is out of this world. She lies on the bed and fixes her serum; her white plastic slippers are sitting under her bed watching every second of her struggle. Her eyes are open, and she is watching the ceiling. I stay there for a while. She is not moving or changing her position. I try to listen to her shoes. They are not surprised; they see this type of patient all the time and they know they will be worn by someone else soon. One of the shoes says, "She is done, she is not fighting for her life, she must be tired.'

Another one says, "I didn't see anyone visit her here. Does she have any family?" I can't stand there any longer; the corridor floor is clean but cold, and my feet are freezing. I know there are many white plastic slippers in hospital, and they have a lot to say. I am glad my shoes are not listening; they might be scared by what is happening to these other shoes, or worse, they might never come back to any hospital. I try to leave the hallway and slowly and quietly bring myself back to my closet. I clean the big, dark blue slippers and put them under the shelves. It is better I don't see them; they remind me of bad memories, how much they say they are flexible and can be good protectors from water and in the rain. I prefer to wear other shoes, shoes that would never leave me alone in hospital.

In my search of the shoe boxes, I see my brown shoes. I pick them; I have good memories with them. When I put my feet inside those shoes, it's like my feet are on a pillow full of swan feathers. They are soft, warm, and cozy. Interesting; no matter how many times I wear them, they always look good. I put them in front of my door and go to bed, getting ready for Monday.

Monday is another day with all sorts of challenges up and down. On the train, no one even tries to critique my shoes; they are built for every situation. I feel comfy and their unique heel that starts from the toes and goes through to the end of my feet makes me tall and strong. I didn't sit today, I was standing all the way to my office, but I was not tired or bored. Today is my day, I am the one who make decisions and whose words are final. Something about those brown shoes is always interesting. It's like no one can get in their way or say anything over their words; their words are wise and strong and do not come out unless they have been well thought-out. No matter who I am facing today or where I should go on site, in the office, or just for a friendly coffee, my shoes can fit into any situation; they change themselves to match that situation. In the afternoon, I walk in the hallway on purpose, and I can hear that my shoes are playing music. People are looking and are admiring them; their final words belong to them too. I remember I paid lots of money when I bought them, but at that time I didn't think they would be with me for long and that they would prove so protective and comfy. I look at my shoes while they are flying on clouds and think I should buy more brown shoes, not dark blue shoes. Wherever they take me, I am comfortable and feel good. I wish could wear them more often, but sometimes they are too strong to fit into some places. I think I will spray them tonight and keep them somewhere special, the same way I am special to them.

I am invited to a party for the weekend. I put aside my little black dress with a pair of shoes that go with it. A few hours before the party, I do my make-up and test my dress and shoes. When I wear my shoes and look at them, I notice how beautiful they are; they have two straps that cross each other in the middle, with five diamonds on every strap, while their heel is around five centimeters. I am sure they will sparkle tonight. After picking my shoes, I put them close to the door and walk in my bare feet while I wait for the taxi. I think, *No one can wear those shoes and not take a taxi*, and suddenly I see my shoes are smiling as if they are saying, "Of course we are not coming with you on the bus and being crushed by those tall, strong shoes." In an hour, the taxi arrives, and I am wearing my shoes. I close the door and take my purse and jacket. As soon as I step out of the building, a freezing wind goes through my legs and feet. I try not to show how cold it is outside and jump into the taxi. My feet are cold, but my shoes are sitting happily under the seat. I am at the party in 45 minutes. It is an amazing night; it's like every pair of gorgeous male and female shoes have been picked for tonight; they are glorious. The best nominee goes to the couple who are wearing the same brand and style but in a different size and gender. My shoes are good too, no one can say my shoes do not belong to this party, they shine, and I couldn't pick better shoes for tonight, but for some reason are not as comfy as my other shoes. Standing in them takes too much effort. I can't jump, run, or even walk fast. When I am wearing these shoes, I have to behave in a specific manner; even sitting down needs to be in their style. I look at other shoes, they all are expensive, and it seems that most of those who are wearing them know what they have chosen and how they should behave. During dinner, I can hear shoes under my table are talking, but even their conversation is not what I am used to. They are all talking about upcoming expensive parties and trips or how they visited this and that pair of shoes. In a moment when I expect my shoes to say something different or at least try to be close to me, I see that they joined that conversation and, surprisingly, all are enjoying their company. For a moment, I think my shoes do not belong to me; I am the same person whose shoes were in the mud and dirt, or whose shoes were jumping up and down. Even my business shoes are different, but I am here, dressed up with my shoes that are definitely enjoying this crowd. I turn my chair to watch those who are dancing. They all look good; I am sure they spent hours trying different shoes on till they picked a particular pair. I lower my head towards my shoes and with my eyes ask them to walk me to the door, but they don't want to go outside; their jeweled straps might get snowed on or dirty. I spend another hour with them, but finally I take them with me. It is hard to take steps with them; they have got heavy as if they want to stay, but we are out anyway. Even out of the party, all eyes are on them, and other shoes are running to clear their way to make sure they are happy. In the taxi on way back home, my feet are killing me, I want to take the shoes off, but as soon as I bend down towards my feet, the driver look at me in the mirror as if to say, *How dare you?* I keep them on my feet for another hour in front of my building. I can't even take one more step. I run to my lobby and take them off. I know I am being watched and probably blamed for this, but who cares? Again, I am home in my bare feet, and no one can take this from me. In my apartment, I put those pretty shoes in their box and put them on top of the shelves. They are uncomfortable but make me feel good anytime I am wearing them. With those shoes, not a single pair of other shoes can even think about saying anything about me or my shoes, and this makes me happy. Before I close their box, I see they are smiling at me; we both know when and how we should be together.

I am in my living room and thinking about which pair of shoes I should pick. My feet are free and pulling my legs anywhere they want, and I am very sure they don't want to wear any shoes, but we have to anyway. I turn the TV on and change channels several times. Suddenly the performance on the screen gets my attention. A girl is standing on tiptoes and jumping up and down without her feet touching the ground, just her toes. She wears white satin shoes with long shoelaces going all the way up her leg from the top of her shoes to her knees. Her shoes are strange, they have a soft plate at the end that she stands on with her toes. I can see my feet are scared and try not to look; they think those shoes would hurt their toes. I cover my feet with a blanket to have more time to watch them. Those shoes are special and couldn't be on every pair of feet. They say we just accept that feet can take injury and hard work and are not scared from dancing on top of their toes. I think that's definitely not for me; their shoelaces keep their shoes from coming off during those movements, and they make shoes somehow pretty. That girl makes dancing and walking with those shoes effortless, but I am very sure she has practiced for a long time. For a minute, I wonder why she would have gone through all that trouble, wearing those uncomfortable shoes for dancing when she could have danced in other shoes. I remember I have seen similar shoes in a museum, they were from Asian history. In old times, girls and women were forced to wear that type of shoes and walk on top of their feet to make women's feet stay small and keep men attracted to them, and now, after thousands of years, those dancers are forced to wear those shoes again – for what? For attracting men or audiences or selling more tickets, or just for showing off their skills? In any case, I know my feet; they prefer not to be known as special or skilled dancers or be attracted to men who want them to wear that type of shoes; they can dance casually and let their spirit touch the ground. We know very well we are not good at dancing, but whatever, if anyone wants us, they should accept our size. I turn off the TV and put the blanket away, my feet run all over my apartment without worries.

It is another weekend and the cold temperature doesn't let my shoes go outside, no matter which pair. I sit a while on my couch watching through the window, but I can't stay home all day. I do some research and notice there is an exhibition downtown. It is about new technology. I think, *At least my feet will stay warm inside the exhibition*. I jump out of my living room to my closet, change my shirt, and wear my jacket. Today it will be my Walmart shoes; I really like them. No matter what mood I am in, they always fit. I know it will be a little bit challenging going outside in this weather but whatever, they are comfy.

It takes two hours to get to that place. In front of the exhibition there is a queue for every section. I pick the shorter line. I am not standing in this one just to get in quicker; it seems they have divided the exhibition into different sections. In one part they are showing the latest improvements in computers; another is for electronic development. I look around to see if I can find a section on wireless technology. While I am looking, my shoes are taking me to a place that they are more interested in. I don't mind, I follow them. In this section there are several presentations and no sign of any devices, and this is probably the main reason it is less busy. I guess audiences prefer to see it to believe it. I stand there for a while to listen to their presentation but suddenly I see on the same side, a few blocks away from this speech, that people are climbing on top of each other to see something. I am as curious as my shoes, we walk fast to that place. I try to stand on top of my feet like that ballet dancer and unintentionally I laugh, because not only can I not stand that way, but there is also no way I can see what is going on through at least five layers of bodies. I wait there for half an hour. Some of the audience get tired and leave, and finally I can squeeze myself into the third row. *Voilà*, now I know why my shoes were so excited to come to this section. The first thing that gets my attention is a pair of metal shoes. They are walking smoothly like other shoes. I can see many of them, not just one pair; there are two pairs walking together. I listen to my shoes; they say, "Interesting, we didn't know shoes could be made of metal." I turn my body left and right and get into the second row; here I can see, between two people standing side by side, how those metal shoes demonstrate strength and capability. There definitely must be some type of technology involved. I move my eyes from their wearers' toes to their heads. For ten seconds, I don't know how I feel; they are robots. Should I be excited or scared? My shoes somehow agree with scary; they think sooner or later they will be replaced with metal shoes. I try to make them feel protected, tell them they can't feel anything, those metal shoes are strong but without emotion, they can't change their situation based on what is happening around them. I am saying these things but I think for the same reason no one will be able to hurt them, and for a minute the picture of a boy I knew in my childhood comes into my head. He walked with metal shoes. He was hurt, regardless of his strong shoes; he couldn't bend his leg, his metal shoes were like one piece of metal from his feet to his knees and were locked with several belts. When he walked, it was like he was lifting all his pain with the weight of his shoes at the same time. Wasn't there any technology behind his shoes? Couldn't they make lighter shoes to match his body's strength? I see my shoes are sitting on the ground almost hypnotized by this technology. I want one of these; they can be around and stay strong when I need them. They don't feel what I feel, but I can program them to sympathize or say something to make me feel good. Sometimes my cell phone does this; she sings a song for me and tells me a joke. I have mixed feelings, I don't know if it is a good or bad thing to have a robot. Isn't this the reason my mom used to tell me that if you have a goal and want to achieve it, wear iron shoes? What exactly did she mean by that? Because iron doesn't break under pressure? Or because even after a marathon run still they can keep their shape without any corrosion? If what my mom told me is right, why am I standing in my cheap shoes here at an exhibition and watching someone else make a body and shoes from iron? Are they telling me those shoes never break, or get old, sad, or scared? Or are they just showing off their knowledge to my cheap shoes? My eyes turn to another metal pair. They are all types of shape and form, from animal to human. They look smart and strong, and I definitely want to have one of them to take care of me but not to replace me. Inside my head I can hear myself laughing. I know it is fear, but who cares? I am a human and have emotion and I like my shoes, but I won't reject it if I am offered a smart robot to be my assistant. My shoes and I walk away from that section. For a second I jump, bend my leg and sit on my knees. People are staring at me, but I want they see what I can do, and those metal shoes can't. Nobody really cares, but it makes me feel better, this emotion makes me different from robots.

During the week I try to watch more shoes on my way to work and on the street. On one of my rides on the train, my shoes were talking and I was trying to listen. Suddenly they stopped. I looked at the other shoes; they all took a step back. My eyes turned around to see what was happening, then I noticed a few pairs of black shoes with an unusual shape standing together and it was as if no one could be around them. They were talking aloud, laughing and even pointing at other shoes. I was sitting but most of the passengers were wriggling away to get some distance between them and those shoes. I tried to pay more attention to them, and there came a moment when even my shoes, usually very relaxed, were scared. These were a type of safety shoes, but how come everyone was trying to keep their distance? Usually, safety shoes come with peace of mind. I was amused by that observation. I got to my destination but I couldn't let go. The shoes got off the train at the same station and it seemed they were waiting for another line. I sat on the bench inside the station. They were walking around as if showing off their power and trying to create a wave of fear. Other shoes were walking around not even knowing they were there, except when they got close to them and immediately they ran away. I sat there till they got onto another train. I saw a bunch of sporty happy shoes jumping there and here without knowing they were watched and any disobedience would come with consequences. Amongst them was a girl wearing high heels and trying to get on the train, she almost disappeared under the line of passengers; they were climbing over each other and pushing the girl inside. My shoes held their breath to see whether the girl could get onto the train safely. Those unusual safety shoes were close to them and I don't know whether this was a good or bad thing, but the same crowd who were pushing that girl and were on top of each other suddenly got calm and let those shoes get on the train first. My shoes and I knew it couldn't be safety or respect; it was mostly fear. For a minute I thought about what the meaning of safety really was. Does it mean everyone should obey without knowing? Is a safe environment for everyone or just for those who are scared? Who draws the line when it comes to safety and danger? Does safety come first for those who wear safety shoes, or is it for that girly girl with the high heels too? Are those happy sporty shoes not safe or are they too happy to realize this? How about my shoes that stay calm and prefer to think about what they should do rather than what others are doing? Whatever it was, my shoes didn't feel safe like many other shoes, but in this, among hundreds of pairs of shoes, they didn't even notice what was going on. After their train left, I stood up and walked away from the bench. Seeing my shoes not letting those unusual shoes make them obey gave me a good feeling and made me laugh. It was a little loud; I guess a few people heard it.

Today, the temperature is better and I decide instead of waiting in the station to go outside and wait. The bench outside is cold but I sit on it anyway. I watch all types of shoes coming, going and hopping on the buses. I see most of the owners are wearing their usual shoes almost every day. I think today nothing is fascinating, not even my cold shoes that are almost asleep on the freezing ground. After ten minutes, without turning my head I see a pair of black plastic shoes cross the street. I can't tell if they are walking, running or dancing; they are not balanced, they get in each other's way like they don't know where they should go, or perhaps they have lost their way. For a minute, I think their owners must be drunk or something, but they are made of cheap plastic material and one of them is torn in the side. I have seen drunks before; most of them have expensive shoes and even don't care if they break this pair or replace it with another pair. These shoes are different. They stop then walk without balance, and it looks like they are not cold. After a few minutes observing them, I check their owner. His appearance is no better than his shoes, but something about his eyes and head is different; his head size is bigger than normal and his eyes are trying to say something silently. Those eyes remind me of a mentally challenged man who used to run around our school. My parents had told me I never should talk to him and should cross the street when I saw him walking. They believed he was dangerous and might hurt me, but I never saw him hurt anyone. As a matter of fact, it was he who was hurt because kids were following and making fun of him and called him crazy. In return he was laughing, and sometimes I saw him hugging them, but I tried to stay away from him as my parents had recommended. This man today standing across the street is in the same situation; no one cares about him, he either doesn't understand how cold the street is or really doesn't feel it. Now and then he laughs, like he remembers something funny. I look at my shoes, who are trying to stay under the station roof and under the bench so as not to get wet and cold, and then I look at his shoes that are enjoying the cold weather. I think, Who really is right, the one who thinks we should keep ourselves warm in this weather or the one who is enjoying, or not feeling? If whatever we are taught is right, how come something is right to do on this side of the world but is wrong on the other side of the world? Even this weather that is killing my feet is probably very normal weather for some other feet. Who says our shoes should not be torn or should be this or that shape, and that who walks without balance is crazy and we are smart? I wonder if no one ever taught him to walk the way we walk, or if just because he thinks differently he is called crazy and if other shoes are scared to get close to them or, like me, their parents told them to stay away because they do not walk the same way others walk. No wonder people are scared to see a psychiatrist or psychologist; we are scared to be called crazy or unbalanced. Because we see these types of people, the next step will be that shoes are scared of us and we are directed to the mental institute to learn not to wear torn cheap plastic shoes in cold weather, not to dance or laugh on the street and to stay in lines for our turn and wait in the station, not cross the street. There are right ways to do things and anyone doing anything else is crazy. For a second I really don't know which one is happier or more fortunate; my scared shoes that are hiding under the station bench or those shoes that either don't feel it or have never been taught. But I can't change anything, this is what other shoes accept, and if my shoes want to survive they should follow their beliefs. My bus is here. My shoes and I get on the bus, and I see through the window those cheap plastic shoes are still standing across the street and are sometimes walking and crossing in front of each other without paying attention to any rules or others' thoughts; they live the way they think is right.

The day after, I come straight home from work, change my clothes and eat. Too tired to go out, I sit on my couch, turn the TV on, change the channels one by one. I don't want to watch a sad story or a romantic movie that ends up with the girl getting back with her boyfriend after the first time they break up and living happily ever after. They are not real and remind me of Disney cartoons that are created for kids. I wonder why we should believe that everything will be okay and will end perfectly. Isn't it because adults don't want their kids to kill themselves as teenagers after any failure? Or do they feel good to tell kids life is great, no matter what? Either way, I am an adult now and don't want to watch those when I know they are not true. I don't mind watching them sometimes when I want to believe lies to make me feel better, but not today. I need something funny, I want to laugh, to feel I am alive and at least for a few hours not to think about my problems. While I am changing channels, I stop on one that is showing a Charlie Chaplin movie. He is walking with his big shoes. I try to listen to his shoes and in my head, I want to know why most clowns wear big shoes. Is it because they give them funny walks and make audiences laugh? Or are they trying to protect their small feet by wearing big shoes? I watch his movie for half an hour. He makes me laugh, then I turn the TV off, lie on my couch with my bare feet on the couch armrest and think about those funny shoes. Clowns and comedians put their feet in bigger shoes, isn't that the reason we laugh? Because we are watching small shoes playing a big role? What is it about those shoes that makes almost everyone laugh? Are we trying to hide our big problems by laughing? Or when we don't have access to big shoes, do we enjoy seeing how clowns make fun of them? Interestingly, most of those shoes have a big head and make their owners walk in such a way that everyone knows they don't belong to them. Why don't those shoes walk straight and usually move to the left and right? Are they trying to tell us something? How come any time I watch those funny walks, I feel much better? For five minutes, I think about my feelings. I am not wearing any shoes; it means I couldn't be thinking of my own shoes. Is it something about those big shoes? I think I know what it is. I feel the same as the clown, pretending my feet are in big shoes; I can tell any joke or make fun of any big problems while my feet are in their shoes, and it makes me happy. I try to remember one time I was watching a clown show and paid attention to the audience's faces. Some of them were enjoying hearing someone saying what they wished to say, but their feet were not in big shoes. Some of them were embarrassed to see the clown disclosing their secrets; that's why inside they were laughing but pretended that they didn't care or that those jokes were nonsense. Some of them, without paying attention to shoes, just by seeing that a clown is wearing different clothes and his face is painted, laughed; I guess they were laughing at the clown and though they would never be in that position or on stage and were too serious to tell those types of nonsense jokes. Amongst this, the most pure laughs were from kids; they enjoyed every second of the show, and this group of kids' parents never scared them away from clowns because they were concerned their kids would be one of them or pay attention to their looks and shoes. I know some kids are scared of clowns; their parents probably didn't want them to know that many things cannot be said in the serious world. Regardless of what those funny jokes and small feet in big shoes are doing, they make me feel good, the way I jump off the couch to eat something, feeling good and small and not wearing big shoes and not having to tell jokes to disclose my problems, not in this moment anyway.

I am sitting in front of my closet shelves to pick another pair of shoes. For some reason today I feel white; it is a feeling of peace and mellowness. I can hear most of the shoes laughing at me now and saying, "What is it today? Are you looking for adventure, or drama, or mystery?" I smile but try not to laugh, this way they can't know which one I am going to pick. I look at the shoe boxes from top to bottom and right to left. I like those white comfy shoes; they give me a feeling of being light and jumping around. Is this why golfers and tennis players choose shoes like this? I know golf players use comfy shoes, but they definitely don't jump up and down like tennis players. So why are their shoes very similar ? Who else likes these shoes? For a moment I got goosebumps. It is a type of fear with pleasure; I saw those shoes many times, walking around in hospitals without any noise. You never know when they are behind you or coming with a big vial. I am sure that after recovery, patients could like them, but during pain and suffering the last thing they expect is a pair of silent shoes beside their beds. I don't know why nurses wear them but not doctors. Is it because doctors are allowed to make noise or their walking tells other shoes they are boss? What do tennis players, golfers and nurses have in common? For a minute I think about this. I really don't know. Perhaps they all have a target and can run after that, but sometimes strategy dictates just to stay in one place and see how far away that target might be. They need to step slowly so as not to make their target aware that they are coming. In this hunt, they could be winner or loser.

Whatever, I don't want to know what they think. I prefer to take pleasure in my comfy shoes. My target is clear; stay away from trouble and live in peace. I can hear other shoes having arguments; some of them are hardcore, rigid hunters, some of them prefer get their target without moving too much, and some of them, like the ones I picked, really don't want to be involved in this hunt. I put on my shoes and step out of the closet to go out for a pleasant day, and definitely not hunting.

Today is raining, and I am glad it is the weekend and I don't have to go out. For half an hour I just watch the rain through my window; it is beautiful when you are inside. I have planned to organize my locker this weekend. I just put on my flip flops and go downstairs into the basement, unlock my locker and move some stuff to make some new space. I don't know why I am keeping some of these things. While I am moving tools, bits of wood and some drawers, I see a pair of long black boots at the end of my locker. What are they doing here? I completely forgot about them. I pick one of them up; it is muddy and dusty and has clearly been sitting here for a long time waiting for someone to pick it up. The other one is clean. I used to wear them outside in the mud and rain. They are made of plastic and are perfect for rainy muddy days. I put the dirty one back beside his partner and sit on the floor to remember why I left them here and why they are not in my closet or at least upstairs. I am very sure it is something to do with what they are made of; it must be something about the cheap material that is used for criminals' shoes in jail, for nursing homes, for patients in hospitals and for workers in bad weather. Criminals in jail are not allowed to wear any expensive shoes and this is the only pair of shoes they have. I guess this way they are told their feet aren't worth better shoes; but how about patients or nursing home residents? Are their feet worthless? Or is this way they are told it is over; this is last pair of shoes you will ever wearing? I have even seen some movies where those who wash dead bodies or perform autopsies wear long black boots, probably because after use they throw them out or, just like me, throw them in the basement because they are cheap and not every pair of feet wants to wear them. When I was buying this pair, there were all types of colorful boots inside the store, mostly for kids. Parents were trying those on their kids' feet, and they looked very good. How come kids wear them under rain, play and enjoy those cheap shoes, but when we are adults, they are just used one time or for bad situations? I see one of my boots lying on the ground like he never wants to be worn again and his partner standing close to him and staring at me to see what my decision is. They know are not made for the long term or for special occasions; they know what they can and cannot do. I think these plastic shoes talked a lot about their destiny in the factory and how temporary they are – bought and used and discarded, and then no one will remember them. They are right; I forgot about them. If it wasn't for those patients in hospitals, I probably wouldn't even remember nursing home shoes. They are all forgotten; someone used them and threw them away or put them in a nursing home or a locker. I feel my feet are embarrassed and my flip flops are moving backwards, like they are with me in this ignorance. There is nothing I can do for those shoes, they have been in my locker for a long time and there is no way I can save them. They are right; it is over. It was a temporary use, and they have to go. I put them in a plastic bag from the same material they are made of and drop them into garbage shooter. I know those who made them knew this would happen sooner or later.

This week I start my day with my high-heeled ankle boot with long shoelaces all along my shoes. They are the female version of army boots, that's why they have heels.

Anytime I am wearing them, I am sensitive to time; somehow they remind me of boots that soldiers are wearing. Their shoes are shiny all the time, with long, tight shoelaces. They can take your foot as high as your head. I saw this in army performance in independence days. When they are together, they have harmony if they want, and if necessary, they can be the most cruel, hard shoes. My shoes couldn't be like them, it is just the girly version of those shoes, but it makes me be on time, have discipline and step with caution. Those shoes are able to do anything they want, but have to follow certain instructions. Surprisingly, my boots are brown. I don't know how I bought brown shoes without realizing it, or if something in the back of my head made me buy this color. Either way, I like them; they are fashionable, they make me taller and somehow a follower. I guess this way I feel less responsibility, and my shoes follow orders just like army shoes and don't have to be concerned about consequences.

While I am wearing those boots at the office, I notice other shoes are looking at them and I guess most of them enjoy how they are following orders. They believe being a follower is easier than being a leader and accept my shoes into their group, but something about my shoes' color makes them different. They are following orders but try to know their steps; they don't step on black stronger shoes or shiny shoes; they don't step on shoes made from the same fabric; they do not follow shoes in certain areas, and finally they stay away from mud and water to make sure their fabric is not damaged. At the end of the day my legs hurt after standing all day on high heels. We are going home strong without showing any pain; we know at home we will have free time to rest and release our pain.

Since this cold weather is not going away, I decide to take a visit to a store that has all types of sporty shoes. The store is divided into different sections, one for use on water, one for hunting and camping, one for jogging and… I try to stop at every section to listen to the shoes. Obviously, because of long-term exercise, they all look good. I walk all the way to the water section. There are a pair of shoes that get my attention; they don't look like other shoes, and you definitely cannot wear them everywhere. They have a long flexible triangle on top of the shoes. Most of them are made of some type of material that is water-resistant. I look at those weird shoes and think about the first person was making them; what was he thinking? For sure he was sitting for a long time staring at animals in the water. These shoes look like fish fins, they can move under water and make your feet move like a fish. It's interesting that humans will never be able to swim in water like a fish, the same way they never fly in the sky like a bird. Is this the reason we put animals in cages, to show them that though we cannot fly or swim in the sea or sky, the earth is our territory and they cannot live around freely? For centuries, humans have tried to take over the sky and seas by making all types of airplanes, moraines, boats, ships, and parachutes, but still sky and water belong to animals. Is this the reason we rub our technology in their faces by building underwater tunnels, bridges and ships like the Titanic to show them now that we cannot swim like them or breathe under water, we can create a space to walk and ride trains under water, and they are not allowed to enter or share our oxygen? Yes, we can make a ship to move thousands of people, or a jet go faster than birds, and we don't care if we are taking over your territory, anywhere you are living belongs to us, even it is a jungle. We pull a fence around it to show everyone you belong to us. If any of you want to live in our home, you should stay in a cage and wait for us to bring you food and water or give you permission where you are allowed to go or not to go. We chose dogs and cats and small birds as our pets because either they are not willing to move far away or they do whatever we ask them. We are human and are able to train pets, it is another power we have and by making pets do things or moves the way other animals are not able to do, make you feel special and different, but you have to entertain humans and forget about what you are. If humans enjoy seeing pets walk on two feet instead of four, you have to do it, and in return we give you food, a home and the honor of living with us. You can always go back to the fenced jungle or inside cages or take risks of being killed by a hunter or from improved technology.

At this moment, as much as I would love to know about undersea living and flying in the sky, looking at those fish-fin shoes gives me a bad feeling about being a human. I don't know why we should prove we are smarter than animals. Is it because we go to school, read books, learn what to wear, how to speak or behave, or because we cannot be satisfied just living with other humans and try to have weaker friends so we can feel good about ourselves?

I notice that in most advanced societies we have more need to keep pets. It probably because we want to make sure we won't forget about the affection we are holding inside all the time, and if we accidentally show them, we are tagged as weak, bad, angry and many other labels, or perhaps we want to share our love, caring and of course our power to pets, because in the modern world we are not able have a traditional family and talk about our feelings easily. When I get to this point, I look at my shoes and thank God they are not trying to show how powerful, smart, or rich they are. They are a cheap pair of shoes from Walmart, the place I can always buy a pair without holding in my feeling. We could enjoy being together and jumping up and down.

I walk away from the water section and try not to get close to the hunting aisle. While I move far away from it, I can see dead animals on top of shelves; it is another way for humans to show off their man-made equipment and weapons to animals. They are a ringing bell to other humans, saying, "See what happened to them? It would happen to anyone who tried to live somewhere they did not belong." For some reason my shoes are running out of the store without looking back. They try not to think about where they really belong, sky, water, or earth. Who knows what is going to happen after they find the answer? We run to another side of the mall, sit down on a chair, and pretend we have completely forgotten about the last few minutes. This way we both could smile.

The fact that I am hearing what is not heard by others makes me feel sometimes it would be simpler to just pretend we are deaf. Is this the reason Van Gogh's famous painting shows he is screaming while he tries not to hear? My shoes invite me to the last visit to the shoe store. I promise to take at least one pair with me when I visit on the weekend. Coming back home, I take my shoes off, sit on my couch and think it doesn't matter which shoes we listen to, or even which one is right, when other shoes take whatever they want from your walking, listening, and wearing shoes. Every pair of shoes has a story, but they are all a Van Gogh painting; it is for their benefit to just scream about their problems, their pain and their lack of this or that. They do not want to listen to my shoes or your shoes; this way they can believe their problems are the worst thing that could happen to someone, even if it is losing a pen or paper. Either way, I try to stop listening to shoes. Like others who try to show their problems are the biggest disaster, I want to be sure I survive and can handle my problems when everyone is deaf. I already know other shoes' difficulties; it makes me try more, run more, escape more or simply sit and talk to my shoes in a quiet place when no one is listening and no one tries to get something out of it or tag me to this or that, just because they want to feel better and are after finding something, anything, in your talk to make them free of fault for their failures or to cover their control of other parts of life. At this moment I look at my bare feet and my two pairs of shoes that are resting at the front door. Their looks are a combination of not feeling guilty or curiosity for our next adventure. I smile and hug my feet. I know it is crazy, but who cares? They are judging us anyway. I laugh loudly; I think if other shoes were watching in this moment I would definitely be tagged as crazy, lonely, overthinking, and probably with a political label. I try to think about other tags but really, I don't know. Those thoughts do not belong to me, I cannot tag someone based on what she is doing in her home, inside her closet or on her couch. I laugh and laugh, put my feet under me and get a cup of tea to drink, turn the music up and I know who I am or feel. In my evil thoughts I say, "I can be that painting too, you know? It feels good."

I set all my shoes up on the racks. They all look good in their own way; completely different, but every pair has its story and gives you a specific feeling. I put the older shoes on top and then the newer. I clean some of them that need it and polish some others. I put a new pair of pain relief insoles inside my old shoes that no one can see inside except me. It has mutual benefits; I feel more comfy and they look better. I put my sparkly, fashionable shoes on another shelf, they are the type of shoes that can't be with my usual shoes. They are to be worn on special events or in special places. They are more expensive and you don't feel comfy with them all the time; you should be careful while you are walking with them not to slip or fall down. I want to take all for my last visit but it is impossible. I look at all of them, tall and short, wide and thin, with diamonds and without, silent or chatty. It is a hard decision; it is the last trip to the shoe stores when I will listen to their story, and while we will be outside many more times, we might decide not to listen to any of them anymore. We all agree with Van Gogh's painting that no one is listening to our shoes' story; they all are screaming and talking over each other to tell their story. Why should my shoes listen patiently and feel for every pair? Who is going to listen to my shoes, and when? My shoes all turn their heads up and look at me. They don't say anything, but we all know what should be told; yes, it is the last trip and after that we will be deaf like that painting.

After staring at my shoes for half an hour, I think my last visit should be comfortable and memorable. I pick those shoes who were with me most of the time, those who feel my pain and happiness, those who stood in freezing weather and when the hot weather was melting asphalt onto my feet, they are very usual, nothing special; they don't have a diamond headband and are not ankle boots, they are not waterproof or untouchable forever; they are like me, they live, laugh, dance, suffer, take steps for moving forward, feel and they know someday will be their last day, sooner or later.

The next day I wear them, go to the bus station and stop there with my shoes that are freezing like me, then get on the bus, and we both stand tall and strong in the middle of the bus and the crowd. After the first 10 minutes, we both feel pain and discomfort and we know no one will even try to listen to us, they all screaming loudly and unpleasantly. At our destination, we get off and walk in melted snow to the shoe store. Before I step into the store, I stop in front of the glass windows for a long time and look at those new shoes inside. I am curious why we pick a specific color for our shoes. Why do we pick white shoes for wedding? Is it because the bride's dress is white and she should wear white shoes, or is it something about the white shoes themselves? White is the color of snow, peace and clarity. I pause for a moment and think, *Those are adjectives we are taught but what is the real reason behind them?* I look at my shoes to try to see what they are saying. I can't hear all their conversion, but it seems they think that the color white is the combination of every other color, and probably we wear it in our wedding to show that we are calm and peaceful and every color is welcomed and could be part of our shoes' color. Suddenly I start to laugh; I think the reason bride shoes are white like snow is that the bride and groom are already in a cold color and there is no need for cold feet as well. Really, it must be something in that color – and why do we mostly wear black for formal ceremonies and funerals? Is that because no light or other color could pass through black, so no one can know how we feel inside? They just see our faces and no one can read what is going on inside those black shoes. How about other colors; why do we call some of them cold and some warm? And how about colors between white and black? What is about the color brown that has attracted me? How is that someone is interested in a specific shoe color? While I am outside I think, *There are some specific shoes whose color is extraordinary; not everyone would be interested in buying them, so who is buying them? The same people who are driving purple, yellow, or orange cars? They want to be the center of attention.* I can hear my shoes smiling; Yes, we agree. Nothing is wrong with that, I like to see an exceptional shoe color or car; however, I know I can never be one of them, or who knows, I might be one of them someday. Inside my head I think it is funny; people who are passing look at my shoes and it is like we are from another planet. But who cares how they have been treating my shoes in all types of situation, good and bad? This time we are ordinary, and they can tease us as much as they want. In the worst scenario, I can wear my silent boots or ankle boots next time and they will change their minds. It is amazing. I still want to stay outside the store and think about colors, but it doesn't matter, why they are made or who choose them, because we see shoes and colors for a moment and don't even think about them later… Eventually, I step inside the store and look at all the shoes, from right to left and up to down. Some colors are getting my attention, like dark blue or red, green and cream. Those colors are coming with memories and thoughts. Customers are all over the store, buying, trying and rejecting shoes. It feels like the Christmas season; we have to buy shoes for parties and upcoming gatherings and perhaps weddings or… I sit on the bench. I don't know why those shoes are talking and why they need someone to listen to them. Are they ignored like my shoes, or do they just want to get attention? Either way, it is not our concern anymore. From today, my shoes and I will be Van Gogh's painting; instead of listening, we will scream. Who knows, we might be heard by someone or some shoes. If we are not expected to be part of this crowd, then there is no need to change our colors to make ourselves more adaptable.

After spending hours in shoe stores, thinking and talking about every angle of shoe wearing, we come out of the store. It is another day of freezing weather, walking in rain and snow, but we try to make the most of it. We both know everything has an end and we will be part of this end too. So what if we yell and scream like others? At least we are happy to know those judgmental shoes that think they are the only ones who have problems won't expect us to listen to them. At this moment, my bus arrives. We hop on, get a seat, and watch the outside through the window. This listening is over, like any other ending.

CPSIA information can be obtained
at www.ICGtesting.com
Printed in the USA
LVHW021229070423
743749LV00008B/520